THE MENTOR AND THE MASTER

A SUBMISSIVE SERIES NOVELLA

TARA SUE ME

PROLOGUE: COLE

The hardest part about burying your past is everyone wanting to give it life support.

That seems to be the norm, I find, when it comes to digging up secrets hidden away in the far corner of a distant lot you no longer own, in a county where you no longer reside.

I should know. I am an investigative journalist. It's my job to unearth those things seen as dangerous, shameful, and potentially life altering. I don't think twice about dragging them from their dark pits and exposing them under a bright light.

But of course, all those belong to other people.

They aren't my secrets.

It isn't my past.

Until it is.

THE WEIGHT OF COLE'S GAZE UPON HER SENT A flash of awareness through Sasha as sure as if he'd touched her. Which he hadn't. Nor would he soon. He was giving her time. She appreciated he wanted to make sure whatever she did was her own decision. But surely he realized she always took him into consideration.

They had lived together for the last year, the happiest year of her life. The floral shop she owned and operated with her best friend, Julie, was doing well. She had a close circle of friends she could count on. And then there was Cole...

What words best described the man who held her heart and mastered her body? How he always made her smile. The gentle way he cared for her. The fierceness of his protection. His ability to command her using the smallest movement of his eyebrow. The way he made her body sing with a mere glance.

Over the past year, their relationship had evolved to its current state. Those in the lifestyle labeled them as Master/slave. She did not, she told Cole recently. To put a label on them was restrictive and limiting and made her feel as if she was filling and acting out a role.

Her submission to him, she said, was none of those things. Instead, it was her natural response to him and how they were together. Therefore, she refused to give their relationship a label. Cole agreed and said she'd given the best description he'd ever heard.

He then spent the next few hours drawing those natural responses out of her in several pleasurable ways. It was after as she rested, safe and content in the shelter of his arms, he brought up the tattoo, asking her thoughts on getting his mark to cover the scars left on her back by a previous partner.

Her first thought was Cole. Did the scars bother him? Did they remind him of a time when she wasn't his and make him jealous? But her assumption turned out to be wrong. They had talked at length about her scars and how she never wanted anyone to see them. The tattoo, he told her, would both cover the scars and to mark her as his. Permanently.

But he wanted her to decide for herself what to do. They had discussed it the night before, but not today until a few minutes ago when he gave her a list of websites to browse, "to see if she liked anything," and told her he'd be back in an hour.

She liked the idea of both covering up the scars and wearing Cole's permanent mark. Her only hesitations were the tattoo's design and the process of getting one. She typed in the first website he'd listed and potential images of art filled her laptop screen. Nearly each one sparked an idea of another.

She was so engrossed in trying to decide what tattoo design she liked best, jotting down ideas, and attempting to sketch out a few, she lost track of time.

"Little one," Cole said, brushing her shoulder.

He whispered and touched her gently, but even so, she jumped at the disturbance.

Cole let out a soft chuckle. "Sorry, I didn't mean to startle you, but it's been two hours."

It had been?

Now she was no longer focused on the laptop screen, she noticed the afternoon light had shifted. She wasn't sure what surprised her more - that she was so engrossed in her search or that Cole had let her go over time. It wasn't like him.

Normally, at his entrance into a room she occupied, she moved to her knees. But he'd yet to remove his hand from her shoulder and she wouldn't consider getting out of her chair until he moved.

"Is everything okay, Sir?" she asked, not liking the inability to see his face.

"Other than how negligent of me it was to let you sit in the same position for two hours?" He didn't let her answer, but moved to her side and held out his hand. "Come on. We'll go for a walk. You'll be stiff otherwise, and we can't have that, can we?"

She took his hand and let him help her stand. She guessed he wanted to talk. They usually stretched inside or he told her to her stretch alone. But for him to decide they were going on a walk, more than likely meant he had things to discuss.

Her assumption appeared even more likely when they stepped into the hall and he'd placed her walking shoes and jacket by the door. He helped her into the jacket and waited while she slipped on her shoes. Even after they made it outside, they walked almost halfway around the property before he spoke.

"Fritz called while you were online," he said.

Fritz was not only an old friend and the man who mentored Cole in his early days as a Dom, but was also living with Cole's ex, Kate. Because Kate lived in upstate New York and Fritz's home base was in Berlin, they'd been dividing their time between both places. Three months here, three months there kind of a thing.

"He and Kate are moving," Cole continued. "For good."

"Really," Sasha asked. "They've picked a place to stay? Just one?"

"Yes, and believe it or not, It's not Germany or the US."

"Wow. Where are they going?"

"Scotland." Cole shook his head. "I don't know if they put up a map and threw darts at it blindfolded or what."

"Knowing Fritz the way I do, which granted isn't anywhere near how well you do, I'd have to go with the 'or what' but I'm willing to bet Kate wore the blindfold."

Cole let out a stout laugh. "I shouldn't have picked that as an example, but I'm sure you're correct. For damn certain he didn't let her blindfold him."

They walked a few more steps before he continued. "They'd put Kate's house on the market and it sold quicker than anticipated. Daniel's offered to let them stay in the guesthouse until their house in Scotland is ready. Fritz wanted to know if we were free for dinner Friday night. He said he'd found a few things he wanted me to have as he was packing up in Berlin."

"Did you tell them to come?"

"Yes. I checked both our schedules and saw nothing." He looked at her and gave her the grin that always made her heart flip over. "Now, little one, tell me about the image searches."

For the rest of their walk, they spoke of the designs she saw: what she liked, what she didn't. She wished she had her notebook with her because then she would be able to show him, but she would do that when they got back to the house.

If they went through with her getting a tat, the decision would be his. Though she cherished he asked about her wishes, she wanted to make sure he realized her comfort with whatever he picked out. And she told him that as they returned to the house and stepped into the foyer.

"Sasha," he said, which was strange. He normally addressed her as 'little one'.

"Sir?"

He took hold of her shoulders and made sure she was looking at him before he continued. "Those scars on your back have been a source of pain, but more than that, they are a source of shame."

She couldn't argue with that. God, he knew her so well.

He ran his knuckles over her cheekbone. "If you chose this, and it will be your choice, I want your back to become a source of pride for you. I want you to walk anywhere, wearing anything, or nothing, and not to think of the past, but instead of me and the fact that you are mine. Forever."

How did he expect her to do anything other than swoon when he talked like that? "I want that too, Cole. So much." She rarely used his name because everyone did, but on occasion when they weren't using a higher protocol of service, she would. Or in cases such as this when he used hers.

His eyes blazed with heated desire. "You want to be mine forever?"

"More than anything."

He drew her close in a crushing embrace and kissed her with a raw and unrestrained need. His rough fingers fisted her hair, and he tilted her head to deepen the kiss. She clung to him, amazed at how his touch aroused her more now than when they first got together.

He dropped his hand to her ass and pressed her against his erection. "Feel that? Feel how hard you make me? I'm nearly out of my mind with the need to sink every damn inch of my cock as deep as possible inside you. To make you take it all. And when you don't think you can take any more, to slide out a touch. But only so I can drive into you even harder to prove how wrong you are. And once I'm balls deep inside your tight cunt, I'm going to fucking master you with my cock, pounding into you over and over until nothing exists for you except me."

Had it not been for his strong arms around her, she would have melted to the floor in a puddle of submissive goo at the husky sound of his words. As it was she let out a soft moan and sagged against him.

He pulled back and gazed into her eyes. She saw a tantalizing combination of desire, lust, and love in his. "What do you think about that, little one?"

She shifted her hips, making sure she brushed his erection as she did. "I'm free now, Sir."

His eyes darkened further. "Get prepared and meet me at the bottom of the stairs in fifteen minutes."

Her body pulsed with arousal. "Yes, Sir."

2

When he wanted to, Cole moved around the house without her hearing him. She'd discovered his ninja characteristics two months ago. He'd command her stay in position and then he'd left the room. She moved because her knees hurt and she hadn't heard him return. Not wanting to repeat that mistake, Sasha remained still once she knelt at the bottom of the stairs.

The hardwood floors lived up to the hard part of their name. After ten minutes her knees ached. She focused on Cole, picturing his face and the action helped. Not a lot. Her knees continued hurting but keeping him as her focus made it doable.

She'd expected him coming up behind her, yet she still jumped when his hands brushed her shoulders.

He chuckled. "Was that jump because I startled you or because you're anxious about what I will do?"

Oh, fuck. She hadn't thought about his plans. "You startled me, Sir."

"Aren't you concerned? Did you ask yourself why I told you to wait at the foot of the stairs?

No, she hadn't, but since he mentioned it....

Yet his hands were still on her shoulders, and he realized his touch grounded her. She took a deep breath. He was pushing her. And further than he'd done in a long time. She took two deep breaths and focused on what she knew.

"I am never concerned you will harm me, Sir. Only that I will displease you. And no, I didn't question why you asked me to wait by the stairs."

He continued her sensual shoulder massage. "Why are you convinced I will not harm you?"

Fear tried its best to capture her in its snare and because

it'd been so long since she'd felt a hint of fear, she nearly allowed it to catch her. Perhaps because she'd been focusing on him before his approach, or perhaps because he was still soothing her back and shoulders, but she didn't allow fear a chance to take root.

"You will not harm me because you often tell me and others I am your everything and your heart and your most beloved." Her voice shook because she didn't see herself as valuable. "But it goes beyond that, Sir. Beyond the fact you don't lie. It's how you prove the words over and over by more than speaking them. Your actions prove them." She closed her eyes. "Even now, your hands and touch whisper my worth to you."

He placed a kiss on her nape and at the touch of his lips on her skin, her body relaxed. Not stopping with one kiss, he trailed his lips across her shoulder blades, his warm breath a separate, but no less arousing caress. Between his mouth and hands, she relaxed further.

"I want your feet on the floor, and for you to crawl up the stairs with your hands. Stretch out as much as you're able. Understand?"

Her muscles tensed again. Yes, he often took her outside the bedroom and the playroom, but not on the steps. She forced herself to take deep breaths and focus on him. After a few breaths, the tension eased.

"Is this correct, Sir?" she asked, getting into the position he wanted.

The staircase was freestanding, enabling him to walk to her side. He ran his hands over her body, adjusting her here and there to make sure no part of her body bore unnecessary stress.

"How is that, little one?" he asked. "Comfortable enough?"

"Not so comfortable there's any fear of me falling asleep, Sir."

He chuckled, running a hand along her back one last time before stepping behind her. He remained silent, and she cursed his ninja skills.

The leather tails he brushed down her back made her breath catch. He was mixing everything up today. First, he put her in a new position and place. Second, he rarely used a flogger on her back with no quick way for him to get to her front. Typically, she'd stand with her hands over her head.

"I had you get in that position to give me access to your back," he said. "But bloody hell, the sight of your ass is almost enough to change my mind."

He gave it a hard smack so unexpected, she cried out. He gave her three more harder ones. "Not another sound unless I've asked a question or you need to use a safe word."

She sucked in a breath and vowed not to make a sound. She closed her eyes and once more imagined him. The tails of the flogger ran down across her back. Not hard. Not yet. Only with enough force for her to feel.

"Breathe, little one."

She took a deep breath at his command, unaware of how shallow she'd been breathing until the oxygen filled her lungs.

"Good," he said. "Keep it up. Not too deep. Not shallow."

There was a sex joke in there somewhere, but she wasn't about to go there. Not in her current position.

She bit the inside of her cheeks to make sure she didn't laugh.

He'd started the flogging light, but increased the force and it wasn't long until he hit her pain/pleasure line. Then he kept her there. Using the flogger as an extension of himself, he drove her to the subspace spot she loved.

She marveled at the sensations at the place he sent her. How long would he allow her to stay? Not that it mattered, she rarely wanted to leave, afraid she might not return.

"Sasha."

His voice broke through her haze of bliss.

Although this time was different. He wasn't bringing her back down. What did that mean?

"Talk to me, little one." His deep voice seemed out of place in her current surrounding. Even so, it commanded her answer.

"Yes, Sir," she said and thought her wispy voice a better fit.

"What color?"

What color meant *don't stop, but keep on doing what you're doing forever?* They didn't have one. Just boring green, yellow, and red. She should invent one, but how did you invent a color when they'd already been named? They had, hadn't they?

She should use one he'd heard of. It was probably better that way. After all, if she made up a color, he wouldn't know what it was. But which one should she use?

"Blue," she blurted out.

The bliss of the world dimmed for a second, but picked right back up.

"That's not one of our colors, little one." This time he spoke softer and he was bringing her down. That was fine; it meant going back to him.

The return made her happy because she'd be in his arms. She closed her eyes.

"Sasha," he said not more than five seconds since the last time.

"Sir?"

He kissed her cheek and she opened her eyes to find

she was naked and in bed, held tightly in Cole's embrace. She snuggled into his arms. This. This was her happy spot. Where love surrounded her and kept her safe.

"Before you go back to sleep, little one." The cadence of his accent lulled her. "Tell me where blue came from and what it means."

Blue? She had a vague memory but it tried to slip away. She closed her eyes, determined to catch it first. Almost.

Almost.

So close...

Her eyes flew open. "It means forever and I got the color from your eyes."

3

***

Sasha didn't know why she was nervous about Fritz and Kate coming for dinner. The couple had stopped by twice before in the past six months and they were fun. Totally unexpected since Fritz had intimidated her in the past and Kate was Cole's ex.

But dinner tonight didn't sit well with her. Though if asked why, nothing specific came to mind. She sat at Cole's feet while he worked. It was three in the afternoon, but she and Julie closed the shop early. Sasha had hurried home to spend a few quiet hours before their guests arrived.

It surprised Cole to see her and he expressed his disappointment he couldn't join her. *Stupid deadline.* She'd smiled and sat on the floor by his desk, telling him she wanted to keep him company. He'd kissed her and whispered wicked promises in her ear before returning to work.

He sighed and took his glasses off, placing them on the top of his desk. "Is there something you need to tell me, little one?" A simple question, but nonetheless a command.

Her stomach flipped. The last time he'd asked that question she'd gotten herself off in the shower hours earlier. To make it worse, she hadn't told him. Both were direct violations of his expectations. After she'd confessed, he'd made sure she knew of her action's ramifications and told her the second time to expect worse.

No fucking way. Once was enough, thank you very much.

She went over the last few days in her head to make sure there was nothing to confess.

"No, Sir," she answered. "Nothing comes to mind."

Hell, they'd taken a shower together this morning.

He raised an eyebrow. "Then why have you been

sitting for the past hour, looking as if you're waiting for the sky to fall?"

Fuck. She'd distracted him. Her intention to keep him company failed. "I'm sorry, Sir. I didn't mean...."

Her voice trailed off as he placed the first finger of his right hand across lips in a shh movement. He said nothing. He didn't need words.

When I ask you a question, your only response is to be an answer to that question.

She dipped her head, but looked at him when she replied. "I have an uncomfortable feeling about dinner tonight, Sir."

He templed his fingers. "Dinner or who will be at dinner?"

"I'm not sure, Sir." She shook her head; she couldn't explain. "I don't know what it's about. I only know whenever I think about tonight, I get an uneasy feeling in my stomach. Sort of like when you find a box and you want to open it, but you also know you won't like what you find?"

He remained silent, but from his expression, was thinking on what she'd said.

"Yes," he said after what felt like an hour. "I know the feeling. In addition, I know you and I value your intuition. In fact, if it was a box, we would leave it alone. However, in this case it's dinner. So we will have it, but I'll be on high alert. I trust you'll tell me if the feeling gets stronger?"

"Yes, Sir," she replied, feeling better, but wary at the same time.

"Good." He smiled. "Since we have a few hours before Fritz and Kate arrive, I'm going to give you other things to keep your mind occupied. Stand up and strip. Quickly."

4

THREE HOURS LATER, THE DOORBELL RANG. Sasha rested on the couch, curled next to Cole with his arm around her. She stretched, relaxed and sated.

"I have to move, don't I?" She teased, stroking his arm.

"We could eat in here, but it'd get messy." He stood and helped her to her feet. Because of his deadline, he'd arranged for dinner to be delivered instead of cooking for everyone himself.

She hated cooking, but Cole did not. Another reason they were perfect for each other. He cooked, and she cleaned.

"What did you order for tonight?" she asked.

"Italian, but if they ask, I've been working in the kitchen all afternoon." He laughed at the lazy smile she gave him. "On second thought, never mind. All it'll take is one glance at you and they'll see the truth."

In fact, as they welcomed Fritz and Kate inside, the big German Dom grinned at Sasha and said, "Someone had a nice afternoon."

Her cheeks heated at his causal remark implying how she and Cole had spent the last few hours.

"And she blushes," Fritz teased. "A pleasure to see you again, Sasha."

Months ago, before Fritz and Kate visited for the first time as a couple, Cole told Sasha he treated dinner with friends as low protocol. As a result, she replied, not needing permission first. "Nice to see you as well, Herr Brose." She glanced at Kate. "You too, Kate."

"Thank you," Kate said.

Fritz shook his head. "I'll never convince you to call me Fritz, will I?"

She grinned. "Probably not, Sir."

Cole playfully whispered in her ear, making sure he was loud enough for everyone to hear. "Don't let him lie. He loves you being so formal with him." He looked up at his old friend. "Don't stress my Sasha or else I'll kick you out of my house."

His jovial voice didn't match the *don't fucking mess with me* look he gave Fritz.

"Cole," Fritz said. "I would never dream of doing anything to cause Sasha stress. Surely you know that."

Cole nodded, but his movements were stiff. "Just wanted to make sure." He took Sasha's hand, and appeared to relax. "I don't know about the rest of you, but I'm ready to eat."

They headed into the kitchen where dinner waited for them, all handled by the company Cole hired. After preparing a plate, they sat around the kitchen table.

The first part of the meal was uneventful. They talked and laughed, and the unease Sasha felt for most of the day floated away.

She watched the relatively new couple at the table and felt silly over the conversation she'd had with Cole. The possibility of something bad happening or either one of their guests bringing devastating news seemed ridiculous. She hoped Cole didn't think less of her, or her intuition.

"Before I forget." Fritz lifted his eyebrow at Kate and she picked up her tote bag from the floor. She took a brown paper-wrapped package and handed it to Fritz.

Sasha almost dropped her fork because as soon as the package appeared above the table, she realized whatever the brown paper covered caused her bad feeling earlier. She gently placed her fork beside her plate, careful not to draw any attention with her movements, and slid her hand down to rest on Cole's knee.

He looked at her, then the package, and nodded his understanding. Across from them, Fritz spoke, having missed the nonverbal conversation. "I'm not sure if you remember, but I kept a journal of our time together while you were in your mentorship."

Sasha stopped herself from shaking her head. A

journal? That didn't make any sense at all. Why would a journal give her a bad feeling? Especially one about Cole being trained. Seriously, what was the worst it could say? That he would be a bad Dom?

"I don't get it," she whispered so only Cole could hear her. She looked up at him, but if he thought anything was off concerning the journal, it didn't show on his face. He took her hand and gave it a reassuring squeeze.

She decided if he wasn't worried, she wasn't going to be either.

"I'd forgotten about that." Cole asked. "Wherever did you find it?"

"Funniest thing," Fritz said. "It was in a box. For the life of me, I don't know how it got there." He waved toward the journal. "Now you can share all those embarrassing early stories with Sasha. I'm sure she'd get a kick out of them. I also slipped a letter I received from India in there."

Cole's face paled. "What kind of letter?" He asked in a tight voice.

Fritz lifted his wine glass. "I'll let you read and decide for yourself."

5

"Sasha, little one." His voice was low and gentle, but still insistent that she wake up. He softly brushed the hair from her forehead.

She slowly opened her eyes. He didn't often wake her up once she was asleep because he said her body needed its rest. But he was dressed up to go out, had a coat on and everything.

Did he have a business trip and she forgot? He didn't go away all that much. Only twice since they'd been together. Both had been over a weekend and both times she'd stayed with Daniel and Julie. Was she supposed to go to their house this morning? She hadn't packed.

Her eyes flew open. "Did I forget?"

It was still dark outside, but he'd turned on a lamp on the other side of the room and the low light allowed her to see his face clearly. She pushed herself up to get a better look because she'd not once ever seen the expression he currently wore. She wasn't even sure she could describe it if someone were to ask her to do so tomorrow. He wasn't angry, but a quick look to her side told her that he hadn't slept yet. At least not in their bed.

"What do you think you forgot?" he asked.

"Do you have a trip?"

"No."

She frowned. He didn't have a trip and yet he had his clothes on and hadn't made it to bed. "What time is it, Sir?"

"It's almost five, so we better hurry."

Hurry where? And who hurried at almost five anyway? "I don't remember us having to be anywhere today at almost five."

By this time, he'd gotten her out of bed and was

helping her dress. "That's because you didn't know about it."

"And if I had known about it, we'd still be sleeping because I'd have made sure whatever it is we're getting ready to do could be done at a decent time of day."

"I don't think I've ever heard you string so many words together before you had coffee."

She glared at him. He was laughing. *Laughing.* At almost five in the morning.

He kissed her forehead. "Go do what you need to in the bathroom. You have exactly five minutes. One second more and you'll regret it. Understand?"

"Yes, Sir," she said walking to the bathroom. *I understand you've lost every bit of sense you had.*

Four and a half minutes later, she walked out of the bathroom and found him waiting in the bedroom. He held her jacket in one hand, flashlights in the other, and had on a backpack. They were walking? Outside? Before five in the morning?

"I'm still asleep, aren't I?"

"I assure you, you are very much awake." He nodded to her jacket. "Put it on so we can get going. We have a ways to go before dawn."

She shrugged her jacket on. "Will you remind me to do something when we get back, Sir?"

"Of course, little one. What should I remind you to do?"

"To make hiking before dawn a hard limit."

By twenty after five, they still hadn't reached their destination, though Cole assured her they were close. They actually hadn't walked that far, they were just taking their time.

"Is all of this your land, Sir?" She had been with him on the day he first saw the house and property, and while she couldn't remember exactly how much land was included in the deal, she was fairly sure it wasn't this much.

"It is actually," he said surprising her. "When I made my initial offer, the agent told me the adjoining property, which was undeveloped, was also on the market. I decided to purchase it as well."

They skirted around a large tree and she found they were in a small clearing.

"This is it," Cole said. He took off the backpack and started pulling out various items. The first was a blanket he spread out on the soft grass, but when she asked if she could help, he told her under no circumstances would she lift a finger.

Thankfully, it didn't take long for him to set up and when he did, he motioned for her to sit by his side. Once she was settled, he poured her some coffee he'd brought and gave her a homemade breakfast sandwich, her favorite - egg whites with feta and spinach.

"This is wonderful, Sir," she said around a bite.

He chuckled and poured her more coffee. "The food or the entire experience?"

She didn't answer immediately and his chuckle turned into a full blown laugh. She still wasn't sure why they had to get out and about so early, but if she had to guess, she'd guess something having to do with the sunrise.

"The entire experience is starting to grow on me, Sir."

His smile was in his voice. "I'm pleased to hear that, little one. Finish up. It's almost time."

Almost time for what, he didn't say. But she finished her breakfast as quickly as possible and then he packed everything back up. Once more, not allowing her to help. It didn't take him long and when he'd finished, he gathered her to him, sitting on the ground, her back to his chest and surrounded by blankets.

It was the sunrise, she decided as the first streaks of light teased the dark sky. What surprised her more, though was when Cole spoke.

"Before you came into my life, little one, I lived in the darkest night. I was lost and lonely, even when surrounded by people. I knew, even though I would never admit or voice it, that my life was missing something. And not just anything, but something very important and vital. I was scared, not knowing where to look or where to go. I searched the world in vain."

He tightened his embrace around her and she leaned

against him and held onto his arms even as he was holding her. Together, they watched as the light grew brighter.

He continued, "Then one day on an unplanned trip to stay unannounced with an old friend, the most stunning woman I ever saw fell right into my arms."

She would have laughed if he hadn't sounded so serious. To say she fell into his arms was much more romantic than what actually happened, which was she almost fainted and he caught her before she busted her head open. But if he wanted to make it sound more romantic, she wasn't going to argue.

"Come here," he said, standing and pulling her up with him, turning her so they faced each other. The sky around them was filled with the radiance of a hundred different hues of yellow, orange, and red. But in spite of the splendor around her, all she could see at that moment was Cole.

He took her hands and squeezed them. "Weeks later, I still couldn't get you out of my mind. I found I had to return to Delaware, even if I was only able to see you one more time. But once I got there, I couldn't leave because you amazed me with your strength and resilience. Then I was fortunate enough to get to know you and I fell deeper and deeper under your spell."

She didn't realize she was crying until the warm wet tears ran down her cheeks.

"I love you," his voice was low and somber, but his expression held nothing but love. "You already wear my collar, and you told me you would wear my mark if I wanted to put it on you."

He let go of her hand, knelt down on one knee, and held out a ring box. "Sasha Blake, my little one, will you also take my name? Will you marry me and become mine in every way possible?"

She nodded even though she was more convinced than ever that this was a dream. But then, because she knew he needed the words, she said. "Yes. Yes, Cole Johnson, I will marry you and not only will I become yours in every way, but you will become mine."

He stood, his face holding nothing but unrestrained joy. "I've always been yours, Sasha. Even before I knew who you were, you held a part of me."

He took the ring and she was able to see it for the first time. It was a flawless diamond solitaire, set in a simple platinum setting. He slipped it on her finger and she had never seen anything more perfect.

"It's gorgeous," she said, holding her hand out to get a better look.

"It'll do," he said, and when she looked at him, it wasn't the ring he was focused on, but her. "It's dull and rather ordinary compared to the woman who's wearing it."

Once they made it back inside, he took her hand and, without a word, led her to the bedroom. He walked her to the center of the room and framed her face with his hands. "I love you, Sasha."

He didn't give her a chance to reply, but lowered his head and kissed her. Slowly. Taking his time, as if there wasn't anything else he ever had to do other than kiss her. She brought her arms up and dug her fingers into his hair, holding him to her tightly.

For the longest time, they simply kissed, their hands

and fingers teasing the other with the pleasure that would soon follow. But it was more than pleasure, for every touch of his lips whispered his love.

Just when she thought she would self combust with the need for him to take her further, he pulled back and undressed her, stilling her hands when she tried to help. She whimpered, unaccustomed to him going slow, but he refused to be hurried.

Once she was naked, he walked her to the bed, and lifted her up, sitting her on top so she could watch him undress. And watch she did. She would never tire of seeing him naked. His chiseled chest, the visible strength of his arms, the way his muscles moved, so full of raw power.

Her eyes moved downward, following his hands as he lowered his pants and then, finally, his boxer briefs. He was hard and ready, and she licked her lips in anticipation of his taste. It was his turn to moan and she hoped he would he signal for her to get off the bed and move to her knees before him.

But he didn't. He moved toward her looking like a predator. The heat in his eyes made her heart pound because now maybe he'd take her. He slowly joined her on the bed, but when he pushed her under him, he slid down so his face was between her legs.

Oh dear, Lord. She feared she wasn't going to able to hold back her orgasm. Not today. Not with how emotional the day had been. Especially not with his warm breath caressing her the way it was. She clenched her fists tightly and hoped for the best.

"Not today, Sasha," he said, kissing the inside of her thigh. "Today, you hold nothing back. You give me everything. I want to hear and feel every single thing I do to you. Every moan. Every whimper. And every orgasm. I want them all."

"Yes," she managed to get out before he continued his task. Given the freedom to come as often and as vocal as she wanted, she held nothing back, and gave him exactly what he'd asked for. Her first climax came mere seconds after the first pass of his tongue over her clit.

"You liked that," he said against her skin.

"Was there any doubt?" she teased.

She quickly changed her mind on who was teasing who, because soon after giving her a second orgasm, he slowly made his way up her body. He was taking his time today and it was driving her completely insane.

But what was even more mind boggling was how gentle he was being. Loving her carefully as if she might break if he was too rough. By the time he made it to her breasts, she knew what it was. He was worshiping her body.

It wasn't like he'd never done so before, but somehow this was different. His touch was more reverent. His kisses more purposeful. She wasn't sure she would survive him being this tender.

Even when he finally entered her, he moved with long and sensual strokes, drawing each and every possible ounce of pleasure out of the movement before starting all over again.

"You're killing me," she whispered. His thrusts were enough to keep her balancing on the edge, but not quite enough to push her over.

"That's the idea," he said and nipped her earlobe, sending a shockwave of pleasure down her spine. "Do you feel us? The way we fit together? The way we move?"

"How could I not?" She ran her hands down his back, delighting in the way his muscles moved with every flex of his hips. "I feel you even when you're not with me physically. Because you are so much a part of me, I carry you with me always."

He pulled back and looked into her eyes while continuing his maddening possession of her body and soul. "You undo me, Sasha. Everything about you."

She arched her back trying to get him deeper. Needing him harder. Something.

Finally, he moved faster and when he took her hips and tilted them, he went even deeper.

"Yes," she said in a half moan. "God, yes."

"Fuck." He thrust harder and, not for the first time, she wished there was a way for them to stay like they were forever. Two beings, locked together as one.

But as he moved them both to completion, she realized no, it was better that they be separate. Otherwise, they might grow complacent and not treasure what they had the way they should.

She could think no further than that because the

sensations he created within her allowed no room for anything else. Clinging to him as her release swept over her, she gazed into his eyes and was consumed by his passionate adoration.

"Will it always be this way between us, do you think?" she asked him, later, when their pulses had slowed and she rested with her head on his chest.

"No," he said, stroking her hair. "Based on what I've experienced so far with you, it'll only get better."

She turned in his arms and felt the truth of his words in her soul. "I can't wait."

6

"Bloody hell," Cole said two weeks after his proposal while they ate breakfast. Actually, she'd finished hers, but he was still eating and hadn't dismissed her yet. He mumbled under his breath, reading something on his phone.

"Is there a problem, Sir?" She tried to see the screen, but the angle made it impossible.

"Just my mother." With a sigh, he handed her the phone.

It was an announcement from a newspaper. Her breath caught as she read.

The engagement is announced between Cole, son of The Hon Cornelius Johnson, deceased, late of Yorkshire and Mrs. Judith Johnson MacDonald Lovett of Hertfordshire, and Sasha Blake of Delaware.

She wasn't sure why, but it came across as a slap on the face. "I'd have given her my parents' names if she'd asked."

"I know you would have." He pushed back and opened his arms. "Come here, little one."

She scurried to him and climbed into his lap, resting her head on his chest.

"Don't frown." He stroked her back. "This had nothing to do with either one of us. It was all about her. I don't know, perhaps her friends have been asking her when her oldest son was getting married. Or maybe she went to a wedding recently and wanted to prove she could do one better. I don't know why she does anything. Hertfordshire? When everyone knows she's been living in Paris for the past eighteen months?"

She lifted her head. "Did she send it to you?"

"Yes. I suppose to prove what a doting mother I have."

Sasha bit back her snort. She'd met Cole's mother once, last fall when her future mother-in-law flew to the States to visit an exclusive spa in Naples, Florida. The two of them flew down for the weekend because his mother didn't want to take time out of her stay to fly north a few hours to pay her son a visit.

"I have an idea," he said. Clearly, all discussions pertaining to his mother were finished. Whatever thought had taken root in his head brought a wicked glint to his eyes. "We should hold an engagement party. Here. And only invite our Partner's friends."

"Are you suggesting a kinky engagement party, Sir?"

"Of course. Any other kind would be boring."

She laughed because he was right.

THE MORNING OF THE PARTY, Sasha jogged to the mailbox hoping to reach it before the mail carrier. In the three weeks since Cole showed her the announcement they'd received a near constant flow of well-wishes and gifts. She held the last of the thank you's, completed moments ago and ready to go out.

"Shit." The lone envelope waiting confirmed she'd arrived too late. She snatched the red envelope and shoved the thank you's in, lifting the flag to alert the carrier.

On her way back to the house, she turned the red envelope over. It was international mail, but didn't have a return address. Odd. Didn't international mail have to have one or was she making that up? They addressed it to "Cole Johnson and Sasha Blake", so she opened it and pulled out the single sheet of paper.

Red. Just like the envelope and written in a gorgeous script was a simple message. *All my best.* No signature, only an initial. A sole "N". Weird. Maybe Cole would recognize the handwriting?

She quickened her step and opened the door. Head down, her focus on the note, she called out, "Sir? Do you know..." Her voice trailed off, and she drew to a stop.

Cole stood in the foyer. Waiting. He took the mail from her. What was he doing? She saw his glance at the floor and dropped to her knees, lowering her head just in time.

"I'm not concerned with the mail at the moment. Look at me," he said and when she complied, he continued. "I've decided the party tonight will be high protocol."

Fuck yes.

"It's been too long," he added.

Yes, she agreed silently.

"You need time to prepare, so whatever you had planned to do before the party will have to wait. If there's something you can't put off until tomorrow, tell me now and I'll take care of it myself."

She ran through her list of things to do and found nothing urgent. "There's nothing, Sir. It can all wait until tomorrow."

"Very good." He placed the mystery envelope on a nearby table and covered the remaining distance until he stood in front of her. "Take my trousers down."

Arousal and excitement pounded through her veins.

It was such a turn on when he used her in the middle of the day. With nimble fingers she made quick work of his pants. Right as she was about to sit back on her heels and admire his erection through his boxers, he commanded her again.

"Get my cock out."

She leaned forward and eased his boxers down. His cock stood long, hard, and thick, ready to use her in whatever manner he desired.

"Sit back and open your mouth with your hands behind your back."

Damn, that meant he wouldn't allow her to touch him. She hurried into the position he wanted, regulating her breathing as much as possible.

He placed a hand on either side of her face, lining her up with his cock. "I'm going to fuck your throat. Your job is to remain still and take it like the fuck toy you are. If you need to safeword, tap my leg. Understand?"

"Yes, Sir."

Without another word, he thrust forward, hitting the back of her throat with a force that made her eyes water. "You better take my cock all the way down your throat. Let that thick cock inside." He didn't pull back, he waited mere seconds before moving forward again. Better prepared this time, she opened her throat, allowing him to push in deeper.

He took everything she allowed and then asked for more. Pumping in and out, giving her just enough time to catch her breath before his cock took it away again. And again. All the while he talked. "Yes. That's it. Going to fuck it so hard. Take it. Take it again. Deeper. Deeper. Ahh, fuck yes. So fucking good."

She worked as hard as she could to keep still and to allow him to use her for his pleasure. Though she'd be lying to say his words had no effect on her. She was so worked up, she feared she might come without him even touching her. But she forced herself away from the edge. Not wanting to earn a punishment on the day of their engagement party helped.

"Getting ready to come." He fisted her hair, ensuring she didn't move and released down the back of her throat. She sat back down her heels. It was difficult not to help him redress, but he hadn't given her permission to move her hands.

He pulled his clothes back on then lowered his hand to stroke her cheek. "I'm pleased. You did very well, little one."

She beamed with his praise.

TWO HOURS BEFORE THE PARTY, she remembered the red envelope and walked to the foyer to see if remained on the table. It wasn't there.

Cole probably put it in the box they were using to store all the well wishes.

But she didn't find it there either.

"Sir," she said as he walked into the living room. "That red -"

He held up his hand, and she didn't imagine the way his gaze grew colder. "Are you ready for our guests to arrive?"

"No, Sir, but I -"

He held his hand up again. "In that case, you don't

have time to meander around the house, looking for an unsigned note."

Did he mean he didn't know who it was from either? She crossed her arms. "But Sir -"

"Kneel!"

She dropped to her knees. Fuck. Fuck. Fuck. She punctuated each step he took toward her with a silent fuck until the toe of his shoes came into view, inches from her knees. She wanted to raise her head, to look in his eyes, and tell him she was sorry, but she didn't dare.

"Do you know the difference between sentences that are questions and those that are not?"

"Yes, Sir."

"Interesting. Tell me, is, *you don't have time to meander around the house*, a question?"

"No, Sir."

"Then I don't expect a response. Is, *how long has it been since I've striped your ass with my cane*, a question?"

Dread filled her body. Why had she pushed him instead of shutting up? "Yes, Sir."

"Very good. And your answer to that question is?"

"Seven months, I think, Sir."

"Pity I have to do it today. Especially since I have to double the number of strokes to make sure next time I ask that question, you answer with certainty."

He didn't release her to move. She remained kneeling, wondering if she could take ten cane strokes. God, she was such an idiot.

"Go prepare the room and get into position," he finally said. "I'll be there in fifteen minutes."

She hurried to the room they had set up as a playroom. Cole learned soon after she moved in that if she didn't want to think about something, she'd empty her mind of everything. Hence why he required her to prepare the room for discipline sessions. Holding his cane made her think about what was coming.

Everything, in place, she positioned herself over the chair the way he required, the cane in her direct line of sight. She took even breaths, waiting for the soft thud of his footsteps. They came, much too soon.

He walked in and stood next to the cane. She watched as he rolled up his sleeves. "This is not how I wanted to spend the afternoon," he said.

That made two of them.

"Tell me why we are," he commanded.

"Because you told me not to do something, and I tried to argue."

"Yes, you were acting like a brat." He folded his arms across his chest. "Did acting that way get you what you wanted?"

"No, Sir."

"I suggest you remember how you feel right now the next time you're tempted to act in such a manner."

She didn't think it possible to do otherwise.

"Tell me why I have to double the number of strokes."

"Because I wasn't certain when my last one occurred."

"Will you have any trouble remembering today?"

"No, Sir."

She appreciated he never rushed a discipline session, and he always made sure she knew her mistake, but damn, it was hell on her nerves.

It was almost a relief when he picked up the cane and walked to stand behind her. "This is the first time I'm giving you ten, but I will not go easy on you. We've been together long enough for you to know what I expect of you and what I will not tolerate. They will be hard and they're going to hurt. I expect for you to take them and to stay still and silent while doing so."

She hoped she could meet his expectations. Abby West told her she loved it when Nathaniel used a cane outside of discipline sessions and added he could make her orgasm with one.

Cole's cane whooshed through the air, landing on her ass with a fiery hot pain that vibrated throughout her body.

Abby West was out of her fucking mind.

7

THERE WAS NO HIDING HER SORE ASS AT THE party, Sasha discovered soon after everyone arrived. The dress Cole gave her to wear had no panties. Even calling the outfit a dress was a stretch since the hemline grazed her upper thighs. Whenever Cole had her stand beside him, his hand always went up her skirt so he could rest his hand on her naked ass. If it weren't for the scars on her back that made public nudity a hard limit, she'd be naked.

After the caning, which she'd miraculously gotten through, while Cole held her, she told him her thoughts about Abby. He didn't say much in reply but as they waited for their first guests, he told her he'd asked Nathaniel to demo a sensual caning.

Because she was under his rules for high protocol, she bit back her reply that sensual caning made as much sense as jumbo shrimp or a twelve ounce pound cake.

"What do you think, little one," he said. "Would you like for me to give you orgasms with my cane?"

It was a direct question, she was free to answer. From her place, kneeling by his feet, she looked up. "It doesn't matter, Sir. It'll never happen."

Cole laughed. "Was that a challenge? Do you think I'm not up to the task?"

"That's not it, Sir. I'm sure you're quite up to it. And I'm sure you could give a lot of submissives orgasms with a cane. I don't think I'm one."

"Unfortunately," he said. "We can't try today can we?"

"No, Sir." Because after a discipline section, she wasn't allowed an orgasm for twenty-four hours. She understood the reasoning behind the rule, but that didn't mean she liked it. However, she was fine with the rule at the moment. She didn't want a cane near her body for at least two months. Maybe longer.

"There are Abby and Nathaniel now," Cole said, helping her to stand. Cole welcomed them, but no one spoke to her. Sasha overheard Abby tell Cole how thankful she was for his call asking them to demo. She added it was one of her favorite scenes to do. It appeared she was on the verge of saying more but Nathaniel placed a hand on her back. Sasha bit back a laugh. She wasn't the only one whose mouth got her into trouble.

ABBY AND NATHANIEL's demo started about an hour after Daniel lead everyone in a toast for the newly engaged couple. Before Abby and Nathaniel entered the demo room to set up, Cole already had Sasha in place. He'd found a spot for her to kneel allowing views of Abby and Nathaniel both.

"It's important you watch more than Abby," Cole told her. "Pay attention to Master West. I want you to see how he wields the cane in this demo differs greatly from the way he would if it were a discipline session."

The crowd gathered soon after Abby and Nathaniel got into place. It seemed everyone was interested in Nathaniel's technique. Apparently, Sasha wasn't the only person Abby had told about her enjoyment of the cane.

Nathaniel joked with Cole. "I'm not sure if my reputation precedes me or if it's my wife's ability to orgasm."

Abby's face turned red. When Nathaniel noticed, he pulled her close and whispered something that made her turn even redder. He laughed, gave her butt a swat, and told her to get naked.

Once Abby was situated, the session started. Sasha had no trouble keeping her eyes on the couple. When Cole first mentioned it, she feared her recent interaction with a cane would prevent her from appreciating the scene. She was glad that assumption was wrong.

There was no way to deny what she saw was anything other than a sensual scene. Nathaniel positioned Abby on her belly, resting on a padded table. Unlike when Sasha was bent over a chair earlier. Nathaniel didn't even pick up his cane until well into the scene. He used his hands. First to massage Abby's back with lotion and later to work her up from nothing to light impact.

He spoke to the group as he worked on Abby, but his tone was lower than normal and he whispered. Everything about the caning: the room's low lights, the silence of the crowd, the gentle murmurs Nathaniel gave for Abby's ears only, nothing spoke of pain or displeasure. He centered everything on Abby.

When Nathaniel finally lifted his cane, Sasha wanted to be Abby. Crazy considering how her afternoon went with a cane interaction. But watching the way Nathaniel's sensual caning worked, in no way resembled what she'd experienced earlier.

When they finished and Cole took her aside to speak privately, he once more asked her what she thought and if she would like to try. He didn't act surprised her answer had changed, but it sure as hell shocked the shit out of her. She didn't tell him with those words, but a look into his laughing eyes told he he knew her thoughts. He smiled and told her to write her thoughts in her journal because they would discuss soon.

He granted her leave for thirty minutes to talk with her friends, and only submissives, he added. At parties she could not speak to men, ever, regardless of whether he was a submissive or dominant, without Cole's approval. Not that she had to worry, they were among friends and everyone knew his rules.

Sasha saw Dena sitting in the kitchen near her husband, Jeff. Dena looked angry enough to burn a hole through Jeff's shirt with her eyes, but he appeared not to care.

"Here's Sasha," she heard him say. "I'll get out of the way so she can sit and talk. I need to ask Daniel something."

Sasha went over after he left, giving Dena a hug and letting her squeal over her ring. She took a seat next to the gorgeous blonde, wincing as her butt hit the hard chair. Dena shot her a look of understanding. "Do we need to move somewhere cushiony?"

"No, I'm fine here." Sasha cocked an eyebrow. "Are you okay?"

Dena waved her hand. "Yes. Jeff's just being Jeff. Normally, I'm okay with that, but when I'm expecting, he annoys me."

Jeff and Dena had announced at the last group

meeting they were expecting their second child. Sasha remembered how crazy overprotective he'd been when Dena was pregnant with their now eighteen-month-old daughter.

"I'm guessing he's not more laid back the second time around?" Sasha asked.

"Laid back? Jeff?" Dena raised an eyebrow. "You have met my husband, right? The tall, dark sinfully good-looking man over there with the great ass just begging for you to take a bite? God, I need sex." She closed her eyes and leaned her head back. "I will die if I don't have it soon." She cracked open one eye and glanced at Sasha. "Not really, but, oh my God I might."

"How long do you have to abstain?"

"We don't according to my OB/GYN. But my husband, Mr. You-Aren't-Biting-My-Ass, says not until the second trimester."

SASHA LEFT Dena in Jeff's hands when he returned from talking to Daniel. She had fifteen minutes until Cole expected her back at his side. Julie and Daniel had breezed by the kitchen five minutes ago. She walked in the direction they went, hoping to cross paths.

Her route took her past Cole's office and as she approached, the sound of someone shuffling papers drew her attention. Was someone in there? She froze, wanting to know who it was before she either alerted Cole or confronted them herself.

"Here it is," Cole said from inside the office. "Handwriting looks the same."

"You're right," Fritz said. "I didn't think it was. Hell, how long has it been?"

"Not long enough," Cole replied and Sasha pictured him running his fingers through his hair.

"Since India?"

If Cole answered his question, she didn't hear. India? What did that have to do with anything?

"First the journal and this arriving today. I must be in a shitty episode of *This is Your Life*."

"Maybe it's because you should have told Sasha before now."

Her heart pounded. Told her what?

"Don't. Not right now. Just don't."

Why did Cole sound so angry?

"How do you think she found you?" Fritz asked.

"Probably that fucking announcement mother had to get in the papers. Damn red stationary."

Red stationary? Cole knew who sent the note and somehow they tied in with the journal and India. Her heart sank. Something Fritz thought Cole should tell her, but Cole refused. And got angry at the suggestion.

She crept back to the kitchen, trembling and no longer interested in finding Julie. Abby stood at the island and rushed to her side.

"Are you okay?" She asked guiding Sasha into a nearby chair away from the group. "Do you need some water?"

"No," she said. "But if you have any idea what happened to Cole when he was in India, I'd love you forever." She'd said it as a joke, but Abby's eyebrows furrowed.

"Now that you mention it...."

Sasha sat up. Holy fuck! Did Abby know something? "What?"

"It's nothing specific," Abby said almost as an apology. "But the first time I met Cole, he'd recently returned from India and he looked sad. What did he say?" She paused, thinking. "It was something like: it was a beautiful place and he liked the people, but he didn't think he'd ever return. I only remember it because of his voice and the pained look on his face. Do you know what happened?"

"No, but I'm sure as hell going to find out."

8

THE NEXT DAY, SHE TRIED TO PUT EVERYTHING out of her mind as she went with Julie to try on wedding gowns. This was not their first time shopping, and the situation was getting dire. Julie and Daniel's wedding was six months away. That amount of time cut down on the number of dresses Julie could order and expect to arrive in time. It wasn't for lack of trying, Julie hadn't been able to find anything she liked. Unfortunately, they were running out of places to look.

"It's times like this," Julie said, searching through the racks of yet another bridal salon. The store they were in was more of a wedding gown outlet, but several people had recommended it, praising the numerous gowns offered. "I wish my sister still worked for that designer."

"Isn't that the truth," Sasha said. Things had been easier when her sister could mail whatever she wanted. With wedding gowns, though, Sasha doubted Julie wanted to shop by mail.

"There has to be something, somewhere I like. There has to be." Julie frowned at the two gowns Sasha held up. "You know, if one of us would go all Bridezilla, I would have picked you over me."

Sasha shoved the two gowns back on the Buy Today. Take Home Today rack. "Thanks?"

"I didn't mean it negatively," Julie tried to explain. "It's just...."

"Never mind." Sasha eyed several gowns to get a feel for what she liked, promising herself she'd find one in half the time it took Julie. "You know Daniel wouldn't care if you showed up wearing a burlap bag."

Julie raised an eyebrow. "Maybe, but I can't even imagine what our wedding pictures would look like."

"As long as you told him to wear one, it wouldn't

matter."

"And the rest of the wedding party? Would you wear a burlap bag to my wedding?"

"Hell, no. Have you lost your mind?" At her exclamation, Julie's mouth dropped open in shock. Sasha waved a hand at her. "Please. You and I both know you would never wear a burlap bag to your own wedding even if the rest of the wedding party did."

"True," Julie said watching as Sasha studied and rejected a gown, putting it back without asking for an opinion. "Wait." Julie pushed her out of the way and grabbed the rejected gown. "This one."

Sasha eyed the bag clutched in Julie's hands. "Are you sure? You tried the exact gown on when we went to those salons in New York."

"No. That one had beading. This one has crystals. The one in New York had a gathered waistline, and this one is smoother." She looked at the tag. "But it is the same designer so there are similarities. It's my size. Come on, let's try it on!"

Forty-five minutes later, they sat in a nearby coffee

shop having a quick snack before heading back home. Julie was on the phone with Daniel and Sasha couldn't tell who was happier she bought a gown.

"It's perfect," she gushed to her Dom and fiancé. "The woman in charge of alterations said she'd never seen an off the rack gown need so few modifications."

They spoke for a few more minutes before saying goodbye. Julie beamed, Sasha thought. Just like every bride should.

"I couldn't hear his words," Sasha told her. "But I could hear his tone. I'm not sure he believed you at first."

"He feared my inability to find a gown was an unrecognized anxiety over getting married. I hope I killed that theory."

"Me, too." Several of their BDSM group's newer submissives had been whispering the same idea.

"Of course," Julie continued, "it's not like we're finished shopping for gowns. You're up next. I'm a little surprised you didn't look at all today."

"Today was all about you, but I looked a little. Imagining which style would flatter me the most. We have time though. Cole and I haven't even discussed dates."

"You haven't? Why?"

Sasha shook her head. "He has an upcoming deadline that's taking up a lot of his time." She debated not saying anything else, but went for it since Julie was her closest girlfriend. "To be honest, ever since that dinner with Fritz and Kate, he's been off."

"Off how?"

"You know Fritz was Cole's mentor?" At Julie's nod, she continued. "He kept a journal about it and at dinner he gave it to Cole. He seemed surprised it even existed. Fritz mentioned him letting me read it or him reading it to me. But he hasn't. I can deal with him being distracted as long as he tells me what's going on. But for him not to say anything, it's like he's keeping a secret. That hurts."

Julie nodded.

Sasha continued. "Then before the party yesterday, we got a letter and the only thing it said was, All my best and it's signed with an 'N'. I tried to talk to Cole but he wouldn't discuss it. Later at the party, I overhear him and Fritz in his office talking. They know who it is, plus it has something to do with India. Fritz says Cole should tell me, but drops it when Cole gets angry."

"Read that journal."

Sasha bit her bottom lip. "How can I when Cole doesn't want me to?"

Julie thought for a minute. "If Fritz was Cole's mentor, it's sort of like being his boss. And if Cole's boss thinks you should read it, I think he's giving you the authority you need."

Sasha didn't think Cole would agree, but it was an interesting way to look at things.

Later that evening, she looked across the table to where Cole sat. He picked at the rice and vegetables he'd cooked for dinner, but didn't appear to be eating. He must have felt her staring at him because he turned his gaze from whatever had captured his attention to focus on her. She sat up straighter, not wanting him to notice anything out of the ordinary.

She cleared her throat. "Julie and I were talking today, Sir. She asked if we had decided on a date for our wedding yet and I told her we didn't. What dates or months were you thinking?"

It wasn't the question he'd thought she'd ask based on the way his eyes grew wide and how his fork stopped midway to his mouth. He recovered, finishing his bite. "I thought sometime late summer."

She smiled. "After Daniel and Julie? Works for me."

Typically, he would have laughed or given her a wink. Not tonight. Cole nodded and continued eating, falling silent once again. It was infuriating.

Finally, she couldn't stand it for a second longer. "Is something wrong, Sir?"

He narrowed his eyes. "Why do you ask?"

Seriously? she wanted to say. "You seem distant lately and I can't remember you ever being like this before."

He smiled and though it was his normal easygoing smile, it didn't quite reach the rest of his face. She didn't believe that smile for a minute. She leaned back in her chair and crossed her arms over her chest.

"I get the impression you don't believe me." His voice remained calm, but the set of his shoulders said otherwise.

Still, she had gone this far and saw no point in turning back now. Even if she upset Cole. "Very intuitive, Sir."

"Are you talking back?"

"Not at all, Sir." She took a deep breath as if doing so could somehow relieve the tension he carried. "But you're correct. I think something's wrong and it worries me you won't talk about it."

He watched her for a few long seconds before replying. "I never want to cause you stress and I'd thought not mentioning what was going on would shield you from that. However, it appears to have done the opposite instead. I'm sorry, little one. That was not my intent."

She nodded and waited for him to continue. He would continue, wouldn't he?

With a sigh, he did. "There are several issues I'm dealing with. One is an approaching deadline I fear I might miss and I'm working late so I don't. The other main issue deals with my past. I don't feel it's the right time to discuss. I need you to let me determine the best way and time to bring it up."

It sounded reasonable on one hand, but on the other, like a huge issue. It had to be major if it both bothered him and he asked for time before talking about it with her. What could it be?

"Sasha," he said, before her imagination spun out of control. "I also mean you are not to dwell on it. Understood?"

"Yes, Sir." Understanding what he was saying wasn't the hard part. It was the actual doing that was the issue. Did she understand he didn't want her dwelling on the issues he was going through? Yes. Did that mean she could do it? That remained to be seen, but she was doubtful.

They finished eating and chatted for the rest of the meal. For a short time, it almost felt as if there was nothing bothering them. Almost. But not quite.

Sasha went into the kitchen to clean up while Cole retreated to his office. It didn't take her long to finish. Cole wasn't a messy cook so she never had too much to clean after a meal. She loaded the dishwasher and wiped down the countertops.

She had to pass by his office to get to their bedroom. Her plan had been to take a quick shower before writing in her journal. It was a daily activity Cole had her do and though when she first started; she wrote in the morning, as time went on, she found she preferred writing her thoughts down at night. Cole didn't mind one way or the other as long as she did it.

But as she walked closer, she had an idea. Undressing as quickly and as quietly as she could, she was naked in less than a minute. She stepped into the middle of his office and knelt with her head bowed.

She could tell when he noticed her only because his typing faltered for a quick moment. Then, just as quickly, he resumed. She feared he might say nothing and leave her kneeling all night.

It wasn't long until he stopped typing and he didn't push back from the desk. At least she didn't think he did, there was no sound of a chair moving. Instead, the first thing she heard was him.

"Is there something I can help you with, little one?"

She looked up and met his gaze. "I thought perhaps I might offer you a distraction."

She had rarely asked for sex. Typically, there was no need. But tonight she wanted to do something for him though it seemed like forever before he replied.

His voice held no emotion. Nor could she guess his mood off the neutral expression he wore. "Thank you for the offer, little one. If it were any other time, I'd love to oblige. But, if I'm going to meet this deadline, I need to work tonight."

Her heart sank. He'd never turned her down before. Even though she knew it was silly, and he had a deadline, it still stung. She blinked back her tears.

"However," he continued. "I would be happy if you sat beside me."

He left the decision to her even though he could have commanded her. It wasn't a hard decision to make. "I would like to stay here in the office with you, Sir."

His smile conveyed his delight. "Thank you, little one."

9

SHE WOKE UP THE NEXT MORNING WITH ONE thought: She would read the journal. Looking back, spending the better part of the evening sitting in Cole's office while he worked afforded her too much time to think. And thinking gave her what she needed to justify her actions.

Mainly, at dinner Cole didn't forbid her from reading the journal. He said he wasn't discussing it yet. Two separate things. She could read all she wanted. She could not ask Cole about anything she read.

He'd told her last night as they prepared for bed he'd be leaving after breakfast to meet with Nathaniel, Jeff, and Daniel at the BDSM club Nathaniel was part owner of, for most of the morning. She nodded, hoping he didn't pick up on her excitement he'd be out of the house.

As soon as his car pulled out of the driveway, she slipped into his office. Her hands shook as she opened desk drawers looking for the journal. It wasn't there. Had he thrown it away or given it back Fritz? Fuck. She chewed a hangnail on her thumb and glanced around the office. Where else?

Her gaze landed on the bookshelves behind his desk and she smiled when she spied what she was after.

FROM THE FILES OF FRITZ BROSE

Client: Cole Johnson

Background: I was approached by Cole, a sophomore at the University, nine months ago because he was researching up for paper on the D/s lifestyle and I was one of the Doms he approached for an interview. I found him to be inquisitive, open-minded, and respectful.

Cole called me again last week as he could not get what he learned about the lifestyle out of his mind.

He believes he might be a dominant and approached me for mentoring. I gave him the paperwork to fill out, knowing that if he was not interested, I wouldn't hear from him again. He filled it out, however, and returned it. I was impressed by what I saw and we made an appointment for him to come and see me today.

Initial assessment: Cole arrived on time and as expected, approached our talk with the same respectful and open-mindedness I noted before. I discussed my plans, my curriculum, and what was expected. He asked a few questions and when our appointment ended, we'd scheduled a start date. I expect it won't be long until he's ready to work with a submissive.

SASHA STIFLED A YAWN. Interesting, but not what she was looking for. She flipped forward a few pages.

As expected, Cole proved to be a quick learner. For our third meeting, I brought in a submissive I've worked with frequently. She has a sassy streak in her, so I don't always use her for a Dom's first scene, but I thought she'd match up well with Cole.

"Mr Johnson," I addressed Cole. We were at the

club I used for mentoring Doms. The owner and I had agreement since I would only be in the UK for ten months. He would set me up with my personal and play rooms and in exchange I agreed to work with the professional submissive he had on staff. It was a win win for both of us and had been working out well.

The room was small, but it was mine and I could leave and store anything I wanted without fear of it walking away. I had staged the area simply today. We were doing a spanking scene, so there wasn't much needed.

"Herr Brose," Cole addressed me.

"This is Neysa." I pointed to the young woman kneeling at our feet. Her head was bowed and her hair pulled into a long black braid.

Cole moved to stand before her. "Hello, Neysa. You may stand."

Neysa stood to her feet and looked at Cole. "Hello, Sir."

Cole looked her up and down, unashamed in his interest and not hiding his appreciation of her form.

"I am aware Herr Brose went over our plans for today, but before we start, I wanted to know if you had questions?"

"No, Sir."

I moved to stand on the side of the room, out of the way, but still in his business. I would continue to do so until he had proven to us both that I could stand further back.

NEYSA? Could she be the woman with red stationary? Sasha dropped her head and kept reading.

It was always eye opening for me to watch a Dom in training interact with a submissive for the first time. Some displayed an easy confidence with the one who gave him her body and mind for their time together. Others were over confident and a few seemed to be downright fearful. Cole leaned more toward the easy confidence but I could see a healthy dose of unease in the unknown as well.

I liked that about Cole. There was nothing I enjoyed less than a know-it-all newbie and frankly, I thought having unease with the unknown was a wise thing. He spoke with a calm tone, but one that left no room for arguing. That was another plus in his column. Tone of voice could carry a lot of weight. Words were important, however, I'd always thought when paired together, the two created a command few submissive could ignore.

He spanked Neysa with his hand. I'd told him at our previous meeting he could use one of my wooden paddles if he wanted, but he'd declined and said he wouldn't use anything he hadn't experienced first.

"Oh?" I crossed my arms at that. "Does that mean you will take a cock up your ass?"

My question didn't seem bother him the way I thought it might. Looking me straight in the eyes, he replied, "What makes you think I haven't already?"

His answer was absolutely perfect and I couldn't stop a tiny smile as I tried to decide if he was speaking the truth. I didn't push him. Whether or not he had, he had made his point.

He needed little instruction during the scene, only a few pointers on things such as positioning and such. Neysa seemed delightedly stated, after, which was something that could not be said of every new Dom I'd paired her with. We didn't talk in front of Cole. She knew from experience I would call her the next day. She also knew if she noticed any red flags I expected her to tell me before she turned in for the night.

If Cole continues in this way, I can see him becoming an excellent Dom.

"YOU LIKED HIM, DID YOU, NEYSA?" Sashed gave a *hmmp* and flipped ahead further than before.

Conversation with Cole about the relationship he wants

At the end of our meeting last week and the beginning of his third month of mentorship, I asked Cole to write his thoughts down on what type of relationship and dynamic he thought he'd be the most interested in. I knew he was a journalist, so I expected his reply to be well thought out and coherent, but have to admit, I was unprepared for what he sent me.

Cole stated he wanted to be in a 24/7 relationship. Typically, when I hear that coming from a Dominant so early in his walk, it raises red flags. However, I've already mentioned several times how impressed I am with Cole and his approach to the lifestyle, so I didn't expect him to want a power trip when he made that statement. I was right.

The first thing he did was to summarize the different potential relationships. The casual, the committed, the occasional partner, and 24 seven. His wrote on each of them and then he made his point for the 24/7. He sees a Master as a person who has given their promise to a submissive to protect and guide and teach. He said he didn't see how it could be possible if you have off times. I somewhat see his point, but the submissive's thoughts concern me more. We spoke about it for a while during his next session.

Wow, he knew early he wanted twenty-four/seven? She wasn't sure why that surprised her, but she kept reading the entry instead of searching for more N names.

"You have to understand," I told him. "It is not all that common for someone new in the lifestyle to look forward to a 24 seven relationship like that."

"I can see that." He looked as if he wanted to say something else, but he was silent for a while gazing off into space. Finally he spoke, "I think..." I could tell he was searching for words. "I think if everything is there. And if everything is right. The couple is right. The connection is right. The chemistry is right. They both want the same things. I don't see why they would want that to end. Even if just for a short time."

"You understand my concern though, about the submissive?"

"That if she's in the mind frame all the time, it might be difficult for her to be herself? Or the concern might be that she might lose her self?"

"Yes, both."

"It would take a good Master to understand and to ensure she didn't do that. She would have to make sure her needs and wants are known. And her Master would have to ensure he allowed her, not *only the way to make them known, but to listen when she brings them up. Because she even though she's a submissive, her needs aren't any less important in the relationship than the Doms are."*

I smiled. "And that, Cole Johnson, is why you will make a good Master one day. You understand that it's a give-and-take and has be 50/50. Our lifestyle is a delicate balance. It's okay if those percentages change during a scene. In fact they should, but the overall percentage has to be 50-50. Otherwise all you have is one person taking advantage of the other person. And yes it's possible for a submissive to take advantage of a Dom."

"I don't think I'll start my first leadership as a 24/7, though."

"Agreed. That's the wise thing to do."

"Now, I'm not saying that if it turns out well, we might not eventually go 24/7." He spoke, had a small smirk on his face. He carried just enough of that playfulness I knew a lot of submissives would like. "I think we'll start out more Dominant and submissive and drifting into a Master and slave relationship."

I crossed my arms and nodded. "I can't imagine it in any other way."

SASHA LOOKED up and glanced at the clock. She wanted to keep reading, but if she didn't want Cole to be suspicious, she needed to do something tangible. With a sigh she put the journal back where she'd found it.

Fuck.

She hoped that was the shelf it'd been on.

10

HE WAS MEETING HIS EDITOR TODAY AT TEN thirty. That's what Cole told her over dinner last night. She'd called earlier in the afternoon and asked him to come into the city. Sasha asked if he wanted her to come with him. Often when he went in for meetings, she'd travel with him and they'd shop for a bit and eat lunch or dinner. Once he got them tickets to a play.

"Not this time," he'd said in answer to her question. "I'm not sure how long this meeting will run and I'm afraid I may not be the best company after."

She'd nodded, disappointed until she realized she could read the journal again.

As soon as he left, she forced herself to wait ten minutes before stepping into his office. Not that it mattered and waiting was stupid, but she rationalized it by saying it showed self discipline.

She found the place she stopped at the day before and skipped forward a few pages.

Though he's no longer considered a mentee, Cole and I have remained friends. As his friend, I have to admit that I'm worried about his relationship with Neysa. She's gotten clingy.

I had dinner with them last week and Cole mentioned he should hear back soon about the job he interviewed for in the States. Nesya looked at him like he'd just sprouted horns and a tail.

"You're serious about that job, aren't you?" She asked.

He sighed as if they'd had this conversation ten times today already. "Have I ever given you the impression I'm not?"

She stared at him for a long minute. Waiting for him to say he's joking, or that of course he'd be

*staying in the UK. When he didn't, she jumped up
and ran out of the room. I glanced back at Cole, but
he calmly resumed eating as if nothing happened.*

Sasha turned the page. It was blank. So was the next
one. That couldn't be where it ended. What
happened between Neysa and Cole? Why was Fritz
worried then and what did he think Sasha needed to
know now? And was Neysa the woman with the red
stationary and what did any of it have to do
with India?

Damn it all. Reading the journal only added to her
questions. It hadn't answered even one. Disgusted
she turned to put the journal back on the shelf, but as
she did, a white envelope fell from the pages. She
bent to pick it up noticing it was addressed to Fritz,
but the handwriting looked very similar to the red
envelope.

She felt his presence before she saw him and knew
something was wrong. Dreading what she would see,
but not sure why, she stood, glanced at the doorway
and gasped. Cole had been upset with her before,
but she'd never seen him angry.

Perhaps angry wasn't the right word. Was there a

word for more than angry? Her mind went blank. Everything flew straight out of her brain the second she saw him.

Why was he back so early?

His gaze shifted from her face to the object she was holding and her stomach dropped. *The journal.*

"Not long after I left, my editor called and said she'd been throwing up all night. Cancelled our meeting. I turned in my article last night, ahead of the deadline. I've been an ass lately not able to spend the time I want with you and I couldn't wait to get back so we could spend the day together." He nodded to the journal she held. "Not once did it occur to me, you would be just as happy for me to be in New York because you wanted to snoop."

She opened her mouth to say something, but he shook his head. "Don't talk." He mumbled and ran his hand across his face. "I can't do this right now. I need to calm down before I say things I'll regret. I want you waiting in the guest room when I get back. There's nothing for you to get into in that room." He turned halfway and looked over his shoulder. "I suggest you obey and not try my patience."

She waited until the front door closed before letting the tears she'd been holding back fall. He had never been so angry he wasn't able to talk with her and had to leave. Her body shook as she replayed the image of him walking away.

11

Fritz rang the doorbell and took a step back while he waited for Cole. When his phone rang less than twenty minutes ago, he'd been shopping nearby, looking for some local honey Kate had mentioned in passing a day or two ago. He'd wanted to buy a jar and leave it in the cupboard for her to find. He loved doing things like that to surprise her. Just before Cole called, he'd bought the last jar from the farmer's market close to Cole and Sasha's.

Cole answered the door, and Fritz hesitated before walking in. He didn't know the details of what happened between Sasha and Cole, but judging from his friend's expression, it wasn't anywhere in the vicinity of good. They walked into the office and

Cole closed the door behind them. Fritz raised an eyebrow, but kept silent.

Cole got straight to the point. "I came home early and found Sasha reading the journal."

"But not the letter?"

"I don't think so."

Fritz dropped into the chair next to Cole. Taking a deep breath, he asked what he had to, "Which means she still doesn't know about you and Neysa. Why you were together or why you broke up? Anything that happened in India?"

Cole snorted. "I wasn't aware *you* knew until I read that letter. Didn't even know the damn thing existed."

"Neysa wrote me. After." He expected Cole's anger and was surprised at when he shrugged his shoulders. "I felt somewhat responsible and called her. We talked."

"I'm glad she talked with someone. She wanted nothing to do with me."

"Do you blame her?"

Cole's eyes narrowed. "It wasn't my fault. I didn't -"

"I'm not here to pass judgement. You both fucked up. I asked if you could blame her."

Cole didn't reply.

"Bottom line, Sasha knows you have a history with a woman you never told her about."

"I planned to tell her, but never found the right time."

"You found the time to propose."

Cole lifted his head. "I never told Kate."

Fritz nodded. "You never planned to marry her, either."

"Sasha shouldn't have gone into my office and read the journal without permission from me."

"Agreed," Fritz said. "And between that and the conversation you need to have with her, you've created quite the shit storm." He knocked on the desk. "What are you going to do to address Sasha's behavior?"

Cole scrubbed his hands through his hair. "I haven't

decided. I don't think corporal's the right direction. Right now she's in the guest bedroom waiting for me."

Fritz tapped on the desk, thinking. "Maybe that's a direction you should look at."

"Keeping her in the guest bedroom?"

"Not necessarily. You don't confine her to a room, but you take away her ability to serve you, to be with you. No sleeping together, eating together, hanging out, or sex." Fritz lifted an eyebrow, guessing it would be difficult to Cole to agree to such an arrangement.

Cole winced. "That's a punishment for me as well."

Fritz stood up. His job was finished. "Which is only fair." He slapped Cole on the shoulder. "I'll show myself out."

SASHA HEARD the front door close for the second time and assumed whoever stopped in hadn't stayed long. Would Cole come back now? She took several deep breaths to calm herself and was unsurprised when it didn't work. How did this get so fucked up?

Was it so wrong of her to read a journal on his office bookshelf?

But...

He was her Master. Unlike Julie and Daniel, she'd given Cole control outside the bedroom. Cole and she didn't live an *ask for forgiveness instead of permission* life.

His footsteps echoed in the hallway, marking the steps he took to get to her.

She kept her head bowed. He was in the doorway. Had he calmed down? Or was he still angry?

"Look at me." His voice didn't sound angry, but disapproving.

She looked up. His face was all hard lines and tense muscle.

"I'm disappointed, Sasha," he said, walking toward her. "I thought our relationship was stronger than this and your trust in me greater. I told you at dinner that there were issues in my past, but we would discuss them when I thought it appropriate. I also told you not to dwell on them. I assumed you would understand I meant the issue was not to be discussed, thought, or read about."

She nodded. Yes, she was aware of everything he said. She'd gone after what she wanted and twisted his words to justify her going after those wants.

"That you waited until I left to go into my office, tells me you knew of my thoughts on the matter." He paused, watching her. "It was also deceitful."

She wanted to argue, to tell him it wasn't deceit. Deceit sounded premeditated and malicious. But even more, she wanted to know what it would take to make it right again. To make them right again. She'd do anything. He could cane her every day for two weeks and she'd take it gladly.

"I hate to do this, but it has to be done." He crossed his arms. "You will not serve me for the next week. You are not welcome in my bed or at my table. And you are not to enter my office for any reason. This will be your room for the week. I'll permit you work, but you will go straight there and back. I'll bring dinner to you, breakfast and lunch are up to you. Maybe by the end of the week you'll be able to serve me the way we'd agreed."

Finished, he turned and walked away.

SHE REMAINED in place long after Cole left the room. The front door didn't open again, suggesting he stayed in the house. Unable to hold herself upright, she slumped to the floor with a big sob.

It was the worst punishment imaginable. If told to write things she hated, being separated from Cole ranked number one. Now he'd banned her from his life for a week. Banished her to the guest room. God, her chest shouldn't hurt this bad. Had he ripped her heart out with his hands, it couldn't have hurt more.

She sat up and sniffled. What the fuck? She was a grown ass woman who had no business crying on the floor because of a man.

Staying in place, she forced herself to stop before she traveled further along that road. She'd come to terms long ago with being a submissive and lived according to her own wants, desires, and needs. Nothing about her and Cole's relationship diminished her womanhood.

His reprimand, no matter how harsh, was justified. Every word he'd spoken struck her like a dagger. She'd fucked up and now she had to handle the ramifications.

That was being a grown ass woman.

The next week would try her, but she planned to face it with all her strength. She'd view the coming days as a learning experience and take from them valuable lessons. After seven days passed, and she knelt in front of Cole, he'd be proud.

With the image of him praising her clear in her mind, she stood and prepared for the week ahead.

12

THREE DAYS INTO THE WEEK, SASHA DIDN'T know how she'd be able to last another four. The last three had been horrible. Cole might have spoken four words to her. The house was so still and quiet; she felt like she lived in a tomb. It had become so bad; she jumped at damn near every sound.

But the nights were the worst.

At night, in the darkness of the unfamiliar guest room, she battled her old enemy, insomnia. Then, with her defenses down, the misery, the fear, the self loathing she worked so hard to ignore during the day hit her at the same time. Unable to fight back, she'd bury her face in her pillow and sob.

As she prepared for her nightly battle, she grabbed the secret weapon she found earlier in the day. While sorting clothes and doing the laundry, she'd taken one of his white dress shirts and hid it in the guest room. Turning out the light, she lifted his shirt to her cheek. His scent clung to the fabric and if she closed her eyes, she could pretend...

SHE WOKE from a deep sleep and felt a presence in the room. Her breath caught in her chest before she recognized Cole. But her relief didn't last long. Why was he in the guest room after making such a big deal about her not being with him this week? And he just stood there. Not moving. Not talking. It was freaky as hell.

"You're awake," he said, but she wasn't able to tell if he stated the obvious or didn't know.

She risked answering. "Yes, Sir."

"I need to fuck and I'm tired of using my hand. I'm going to use you instead."

Yes, finally! She hadn't thought he could go all week without her. He wanted her back. Thank goodness.

"Before you get excited, this changes nothing." He sounded distant. Not like her Cole at all. "You're a hole for my cock. That's all. You're not to talk, moan, or make any noise. Stay still unless I tell you otherwise and you sure as hell better not come."

Just that quickly, she was back to hopeless. He moved and the low light in the hallway revealed he was naked.

"Bend over, facing the bed. The last thing I want to see while I'm fucking is your face."

It would have hurt less if he slapped her. She bit back the tears, refusing to let them fall. If this was all he wanted, this was what she'd give him. He might act like he believed the cold, harsh words, but his body couldn't lie. Once he touched her, his fingers would speak of his love.

She shoved his shirt under her pillow and scrambled to get up and over the bed. He'd forbidden her from wearing clothes to bed and she'd assumed that hadn't changed just because they weren't sharing one.

Stepping behind her without a word, he pushed her head deep into the bedcovers.

She waited, every breath anticipating his touch: the warmth of his palm cupping her breast, his lips teasing the line of her spine, and his knowledgeable fingertips along her inner thighs making her burn for him.

That wasn't his plan for tonight. She braced herself as he pushed two fingers in her and cursed.

She wasn't wet.

At all.

She heard him spit and his cock replaced his fingers at her entrance and pushed. Aware of his size, he'd never entered her without making sure she was ready. The pain of him taking her when she wasn't aroused hurt more than she expected. She bit into the sheet, her body a massive knot of tension while his cock tried in vain to penetrate her.

He mumbled under his breath, pulled back, and spit again, ready to try once more. Her body couldn't take it, he'd never be able to fuck her. But a chill ran down her spine. He could. He was stronger and able to both hold her down and force her at the same time.

She couldn't be with this Cole. The one void of emotion. If he showed a hint of anything... maybe. But not like this.

He grabbed her hips and thrust inside.

She couldn't breathe. "Red," she gasped but not loud enough for him to hear. "Red," she tried again. He didn't stop. "Red!" She screamed and kicked, desperate to get away.

"Sasha."

"Red!"

"I have you, little one. No one will hurt you."

You are. She didn't know if she said it in her mind or out loud.

"Oh, God. Sasha. Don't. Please come back."

Her eyes flew open. Where was she? Who was she with? She tried to take a deep breath to calm down, but all she did was choke. *Another one. Just try.* She inhaled and filled her lungs. *That's it. Big exhale.* She exhaled with a whoosh. *Good. Once more.*

She realized with a start she wasn't talking to herself, rather she was in someone's lap and they were helping her calm down.

"Take another deep breath, little one."

Cole?

She didn't want to look at him and see the nothing face, but his voice differed from moments before. Unable to stop herself she lifted her head. His nothing face was gone. One filled with concern and sorrow in its place.

And he wore a tee-shirt and boxers.

She twisted to get a better look. "Cole?"

A tear ran down his cheek. "Yes, my love."

HE CARRIED her back to their bedroom, where he put her on the bed and joined her, pulling her on his lap and covering her with blankets. For over an hour they stayed like that, not talking, not sleeping, just being.

As the dawn began at to peek in through the windows, he spoke.

"I need to tell you about her."

Sasha nodded.

He spoke of himself, the university kid who wanted to learn about kink and the German Dom who would mentor him. He spoke of the first submissive he'd been with and how he became enamored with her. How after his mentorship and against the advice of his friend, Fritz, he continued to see that submissive, Neysa.

They hadn't been dating long when he realized they'd never work, but he didn't break up with her because he was looking for a job in the States. Before transferring to Oxford, he'd attended university in America and fell in love with both the country and her people. It had always been his plan to move back and he'd never kept that a secret.

Neysa was in graduate school, many of her family members lived in the UK, and she'd told him numerous times she had no interest in moving to America.

The day he told her he'd accepted a job in New York, she broke down and told him she was pregnant. He was shocked because they had discussed children in the past. She knew he didn't want any. He accused her of purposely getting pregnant. She became inconsolable, begging him to help her, and that her parents would disown her.

"I should have handled the situation better and it pains me to admit this, but I told her to get an abortion, that I wasn't staying in England and nothing and no one would stop me. I left her that night. Six weeks later, she sent me an email telling me she'd miscarried. I was already living in New York. We'd have been miserable if we stayed together. I'd resent her for making me give up my dreams and she'd resent me for not loving her. But even knowing that I should have handled it better."

Sasha sat in stunned silence. Perhaps this was another nightmare and she'd wake up to find the Cole she knew, the man she'd fallen for.

Cole didn't appear to notice how stiff and tense she was because he continued. "When I went to India after Kate and I broke up, Neysa was there visiting family. It wasn't planned, neither one of us knew the other would be there."

He paused and took a deep breath. "We had dinner together and ended up talking for hours. I was finally able to apologize for my actions and words so many years ago. She admitted she'd skipped her birth control pills on purpose. It shouldn't have happened. I should have stopped it, but we kissed and I took her back to my hotel room. We had an ugly fight the next morning because I thought she knew it was a one night thing. But she saw it as fate giving us another chance and told me no matter where I went she'd find me because we were meant to be together.

"That was the last I heard until the note arrived in the post the other day. I guess she saw our engagement announcement."

So many emotions and questions were running through Sasha's head, she had no idea what to say first. She pushed herself from him and decided to start at the beginning. "Let me make sure I have this right. You tell the woman you got pregnant to get an abortion and then you leave her and move to a different country? She sends you an email after a few weeks and you consider yourself lucky because she miscarried?"

"I never said I felt -"

"Don't interrupt me!" Sasha's body shook with rage. "Then years later, after a chance meeting, you fuck her and leave again? And now she knows where *I* live?"

Cole remained silent.

"Who are you?" She whispered. "If I got pregnant accidentally, would you leave me, too?"

She didn't wait for him to answer. She climbed off the bed, taking the blanket with her.

"No, Sasha," he called. "Wait. Where are you going?"

"Back to the guest room." She turned to make sure he knew she was serious. "Suddenly, the idea of four more days without you doesn't feel like a punishment."

13

JULIE RAISED HER EYEBROW AT SASHA's entrance the following day. Sasha held her hand up before her friend could ask a question. "Don't ask, I'm not discussing."

"I respect that," Julie said. "But for the record, Bad Ass Sasha beats Mopey and Depressed Sasha hands down."

"Thanks. I think."

"And if Bad Ass Sasha would like to use her powers constructively, I have a few delinquent corporate accounts that need to be called." Julie held up invoices.

Sasha grabbed them and headed toward the back. "On it."

Julie had been out of the office the day before and missed Bad Ass Sasha's debut, not that her business partner missed anything. Sasha had spent most of the day growling at anyone unfortunate enough to come in contact with her. At least today she could do something useful. Calling delinquent accounts hadn't crossed her mind yesterday. Though that was probably for the best. No doubt she would've bitten the head off anybody she contacted and they would never do business with them again.

She'd finished three calls and was looking through the details of the fourth and last when Julie popped her head into the room.

"Someone's here to see you."

Julie would have told her if it was Cole. Thinking it was business related, she stepped into their main room and froze at the man standing and waiting.

"Fritz," she said.

He smiled. "No Herr Brose today?"

She wrinkled her nose. "Doesn't feel like a Herr Brose kind of day."

"I'd like a few minutes to talk with you. Can we walk outside?"

She narrowed her eyes. "Did he send you?"

"No and he'd kick my ass into next week if he knew I was here. But he did fill me in."

"I'll give you five minutes." She looked over her shoulder and told Julie, "I'll be back in a few."

They'd only taken a few steps when Fritz spoke. "I needed to come and apologize for my part in what happened between Cole and Neysa."

"What?" She asked, because that made no sense.

"You, perhaps more so than many submissives, acutely know that Doms are not perfect. Did you ever read the letter Neysa sent me? The one in the white envelope?"

She shook her head. Truthfully, she'd forgotten about it.

"She sent it a few weeks after Cole left India. She was

very straightforward and told me she'd forgiven Cole because she realized finally he wasn't the right man for her and never would be. Instead she blamed me."

"You?" Sasha stopped walking. "Why you of all people?"

He guided her to a deserted bench nearby, and they sat down. "Of the three of us, I was the one with the most lifestyle experience and I should have known better. I knew she wanted to settle down, and I knew Cole had no intention of remaining in the UK. I could see her point."

"I'm sorry, Sir, but that sounds like utter and complete horse shit. Are you also to blame because she decided to skip her pills? Are you to blame that Cole's dream of living in the US blinded him to all responsibility?"

"No but -"

"There's no but." She interrupted him. "We're not perfect people so we're not going to do perfect things. But it's those imperfections that make us who we are. So maybe we should just agree to be imperfect together."

Fritz tried to say something, but she stopped him because she'd suddenly remembered an important but untried truth she once spoke. "Sorry to keep interrupting, Sir, but I need to speak to someone urgently."

Fritz's eyes danced with merriment. "And when shall I tell Julie to expect you?"

"Tomorrow," she answered with a laugh.

SHE FOUND Cole sitting outside on their back deck, his favorite place to sit and think. Moving as quietly as possible, she sat at his feet and smiled when he cried her name in surprise because he wasn't the only one with ninja skills.

He didn't ask her any questions, so she spoke. "Remember when I told you I loved all your parts because they all made you who you are?" At his nod, she continued, "as much as I meant that when I said it, there's no way it could have been true because I didn't know all of your parts then. Even more, I didn't dislike any of your parts at that time."

His expression was guarded. "And now that you know of parts you dislike?"

She came to her knees and leaned forward, resting her hands on his. "I still mean it. All your past, even the parts I dislike, played a role in making who you are today. The you of today is different, you've learned and matured. Better than most, I'd add."

He reached out and brushed her cheek with his fingertips. "If you happened to get pregnant unexpectedly, I would never leave or suggest you get an abortion. I'm not that selfish boy anymore."

"And I'm not that girl."

"No, you're not. Do you know who you are?"

She climbed into his lap. "I'm your Sasha."

He pulled her close. "You're so much more."

14

Sasha pretended as though she wasn't anxious about Cole's plans for the afternoon. *Cole, me, and a cane. Nothing to worry over.* She shook her head. *What was I thinking when I agreed to this?*

She knelt naked outside a spare room on their second floor that before today they'd used as storage. Three weeks had passed since the nightmare that still spooked her, but their relationship was stronger than ever.

The door to the room opened and Cole stepped into the hallway. His gaze fell on her. "I can hear your thoughts from the other room, little one," he said. "Would you prefer not to do this?"

She debated telling him she'd changed her mind and could not go forward. But the truth was she wanted to do at least one scene like what she'd seen with Abby and Nathaniel.

"Trust me, little one," he said. "You will enjoy this." He held out his hand, and she took hold. His touch calmed her racing heart.

They walked in the room together and her jaw dropped at the changes since the last time she'd seen the room. He had removed the storage boxes. The low light of gleaming candles sparkled and danced along the shadows on the walls. Spicy lavender filled the air. And in the middle of it was a large massage table with numerous blankets and pillows piled nearby. How different from the cold and harsh setting of a discipline session. Her breathing came easier.

Cole ran his hand down her back. "Okay to continue?"

"Yes," she replied, wanting to see and experience more.

Knowing her the way he did, he let her stand for a few minutes, looking at everything, and settling.

"When you're ready, you can get on the table, face down. Only when you're ready. No need to rush."

He would never push her too fast. Letting her approach new experiences at her pace proved how safe she was with him. It made her want to continue with the scene even more.

She moved to get on the table and it wasn't long before Cole stood behind her. He covered her body with warm towels and placed pillows around her, making sure she was comfortable. Soft music played from overhead. Even seeing Abby and Nathaniel's scene had not prepared her for this.

Ever so gently, his hands rested on her shoulders. "Still okay?"

"Yes, Sir."

"Breathe," he said.

She obeyed, inhaling deeply.

"Exhale."

He matched his breathing to hers and the intensity of being still and breathing in unison together amazed her. Time slowed during those few minutes when all they did was breathe. His hands rested on her shoulders. Not doing anything. Proving with his touch he remained by her side.

His hands slid under the blankets and with gentle touches, he massaged her muscles. She wasn't aware of when he removed the blankets, only that at some point they were gone. He worked out the tension in her back with a soothing touch allowing her to sink into the bliss of her surroundings.

She hummed in pleasure when the massage evolved to his fingers dancing like raindrops along her spine. The raindrops expanded, traveling across the expanse of her back. They would switch and go in another direction, she tried to anticipate their path and failed. She gave up and let herself go.

"Yes," he said above her and the rain became heavier. Pounding her into the warmth and softness of the table. She sighed, delighted to learn how good rain felt. Over and over until the rain became a song and she the piano he played it on.

Still she soared because his song allowed her to fly. Higher she went, and she realized she'd been wrong. She wasn't his piano, she was his song. The truth hit her in a cacophony of sensations. Unexpected pleasure rippled throughout her body, leaving her aroused and needy in its wake.

"Green," she begged, wanting more.

It came again and again, bringing wave after wave of longing. She lifted her hips to catch it, but it evaded her.

"Please." She had to have it. "Green. Green."

Everything stilled.

Silence.

Had she done or said something wrong? "Please," she whispered. "Please."

It came one last time, and she screamed as the most powerful orgasm she'd ever had shook her body.

SHE AWOKE IN STAGES.

First the comfort of his arms. She smiled and snuggled closer. His warm chuckle was the second. The taste of his lips, third.

"Tell me," he said, teasing. "Was it every bit as horrid and awful as you thought?"

"Of course not," she said and he gave her his smug *I told you so* grin, *Cocky, bastard.* "I don't believe you used a cane one time during that scene."

"You don't?"

"No, Sir."

"What do you think had you screaming *green* and then made you come so hard, it nearly made *my* eyes cross?"

That had been a cane? "Magic Dom tools?"

He laughed so hard, he shook the bed. "Yes, we'll go with that. It was a magic Dom tool."

She shifted in his arms and smiled. "I think your other magic Dom tool is jealous. I better give it a kiss."

He mumbled something about her being the death of him, but he didn't stop her. The thought struck her as she tugged down his pants, she had nothing to fear about going through difficult times with Cole. They only made the good times better.

EPILOGUE: COLE

FROM THE PERSONAL JOURNAL OF COLE JOHNSON

I don't remember the weather on our wedding day. I mention it only because Sasha fretted over the potential for rain during the days leading up to our big event.

For all I remember, it rained. However, the pictures prove otherwise.

For what it's worth, I don't remember the food either. Or the music or the flowers.

No, when I remember our wedding day, all that comes to mind is my Sasha.

I'm standing at the front of the church, the doors to

the back open, she steps through, and walks toward me. At first I can't see her for the happy tears blurring my vision. But as she grows closer, I see her radiant smile. The joy and happiness exuding from her and touching everyone in the church. And her love for me nearly drops me to my knees.

She found her wedding dress in one day. Julie told her she was mad, but Sasha insisted there was no need to keep looking. I laughed when they told me. When my woman knows what she wants, she knows what she wants.

I couldn't see the gown because of ridiculous superstitions. My first glimpse occurs as I'm surrounded by friends and family while my future walks down the aisle to meet me. I'm sure they see the big sappy grin on my face and realize I'm a love-struck bastard, but I don't care. She is the most stunning woman who ever existed. And she's mine.

She arrives to my side and I'm nearly struck down by an image of the first time I saw her. What a contrast to the woman beside me. The Sasha then lived fearful and shy. She was afraid. Timid. And buried in a shell deep within herself, refusing to let anyone inside. The woman beside me is fierce. She is powerful and loves deeply with a passion that ignites something within me every time I look at her.

She is incredible. And she is mine.

Our ceremony is traditional, though she wears her collar and her vows include 'obey'. I'm amazed as I say my own vows and repeat after the clergyman the words binding me to her. I feel bad because she's getting the rotten end of this deal. She doesn't mind. She loves me with all my faults, failures, and shortcomings. She is my angel, my salvation, and my forever.

On our wedding day, she has not yet gotten the tattoo on her back. We're still looking for the perfect image. Make no mistake however, she is mine. I am hers. And no one will come between us. Ever.

I'm confident and secure in our relationship, because now I know we have no secrets from each other, no hidden past, no shameful memories unshared. We have seen the best and the worst of each other and we remain together. She is my rock. My fortress. My shelter.

On our wedding night, when she can no longer evade sleep, I stay awake and watch while she sleeps in my arms. I watch her breathing, the simple movement of her chest, the gentle flutter of her eyelids, and the sweet smile she wears even in sleep. I'm not worthy of this woman. My wife.

But everyday I try to be.

ACKNOWLEDGMENTS

Elle, you rock my socks. Seriously, this story wouldn't exist if it wasn't for you. I know it's not anywhere close to what we discussed three or four years ago (OMG, has it been THAT long) but you know how Cole is...

Mr. Sue Me, you rock everything else.

For readers wanting to see the details of Abby's first conversation with Cole, it's in the first chapter of THE EXHIBITIONIST. When I wrote that part, I was under the assumption whatever happened in India would be discussed in THE MASTER.

Both Cole and Sasha vetoed me.

ABOUT THE AUTHOR

NEW YORK TIMES/USA TODAY BESTSELLING AUTHOR

Even though she graduated with a degree in science, Tara knew she'd never be happy doing anything other than writing. Specifically, writing love stories.

She started with a racy BDSM story and found she was not quite prepared for the unforeseen impact it would have. Nonetheless, she continued and The Submissive Series novels would go on to be both New York Times and USA Today Bestsellers. One of those, THE MASTER, was a 2017 RITA finalist for Best Erotic Romance.

Now she is focusing on new contemporary romances that allow her the freedom to write and publish on her own schedule.

www.tarasueme.com

Master Professor

Headmaster

BACHELOR INTERNATIONAL:

American Asshole

OTHER:

Her Last Hello

The Date Dare

WRITING AS TARA THOMAS:

Shattered Fear*

Hidden Fate*

Twisted End*

Darkest Night

Deadly Secret

Broken Promise

*eNovella

Made in the USA
Las Vegas, NV
19 February 2021